SPINE SHIVERS

SPINE SHIVERS IS PUBLISHED BY STONE ARCH BOOKS,
A CAPSTONE IMPRINT
1710 ROE CREST DRIVE
NORTH MANKATO, MINNESOTA 56003
WWW.MYCAPSTONE.COM

LIBRARY OF CONGRESS CATALOGING-IN-PUBLICATION DATA

NAMES: DARKE, J. A., AUTHOR. | DARKE, J. A. SPINE SHIVERS.
TITLE: DO NOT WATCH / BY J.A. DARKE.
DESCRIPTION: NORTH MANKATO, MINNESOTA : STONE ARCH BOOKS, AN IMPRINT OF

 CAPSTONE PRESS, [2017] | SERIES: SPINE SHIVERS |

SUMMARY: SAM'S FATHER RUNS AN ANTIQUE STORE SPECIALIZING IN BIZARRE AND UNIQUE
COLLECTIBLES, SO BUYING THE DESK OF A DECEASED HORROR MOVIE DIRECTOR, AND FINDING AN
OLD VIDEOTAPE LABELED "THE GAUNT MAN, ONLY COPY, DO NOT WATCH" IS NOT A SURPRISE--
BUT WHEN SAM AND HIS FRIENDS DO WATCH THE TAPE, THEY ARE HORRIFIED TO REALIZE THEY
HAVE RELEASED THE GAUNT MAN INTO THE WORLD.

IDENTIFIERS: LCCN 2015046968 | ISBN 9781496530714 (LIBRARY BINDING) | ISBN
 9781496530738 (PBK.) | ISBN 9781496530752 (EBOOK (PDF))

SUBJECTS: LCSH: HORROR TALES. | VIDEO TAPES--JUVENILE FICTION. |
 MONSTERS--JUVENILE FICTION. | ANTIQUE DEALERS--JUVENILE FICTION. | MOTION
 PICTURE PRODUCERS AND DIRECTORS--JUVENILE FICTION. | CYAC: HORROR STORIES.
 | VIDEO TAPES--FICTION. | MONSTERS--FICTION. | PRODUCERS AND
 DIRECTORS--FICTION. | GSAFD: HORROR FICTION.

CLASSIFICATION: LCC PZ7.1.D33 DO 2017 | DDC 813.6--DC23
LC RECORD AVAILABLE AT HTTP://LCCN.LOC.GOV/2015046968

COVER ILLUSTRATION BY NEIL EVANS
DESIGN BY HILARY WACHOLZ

Printed and bound in China.
007705

DO NOT WATCH

BY J. A. DARKE

TEXT BY BRANDON TERRELL

ILLUSTRATED BY NEIL EVANS

STONE ARCH BOOKS
a capstone imprint

TABLE OF CONTENTS

CHAPTER 1

Sam Valentine had spent his entire life surrounded by weirdness. That was what happened when your dad ran an antique store that specialized in bizarre collectibles. You opened boxes containing carefully wrapped things like the diary of a woman who claimed she could speak to the dead. You pulled from packing peanuts a metal urn containing the ashes of a serial killer. You dusted shelves that held ceramic angels and devils and Bigfoot-shaped salt and pepper shakers.

And sometimes, you rode in a pickup truck, making your way through countryside, small towns, and other forgotten places to find a valuable antique. Which was exactly what Sam was doing. It was an unusually hot Saturday afternoon in May, and he and his dad were on their way to the house of a dead movie director to pick up some things his dad bought on the Internet. Sam rolled his window down and felt the wind whip through his hair.

"Sandwich?" Sam's dad asked. He nodded toward a red cooler that sat between them on the front seat. Inside were cans of soda and two sandwiches wrapped in wax paper. "What's a road trip without sandwiches? Am I right?"

His dad smiled from ear to ear. Sam knew his dad loved his life. And as strange as that life was, Sam had no objections. He enjoyed spending time with his dad. Sam and his friends hung out at the store often.

His best friend Olivia was dying to work there one day. She hoped to see something supernatural, inspecting every old locket or jewelry box that passed through the store.

Sam reached into the cooler and pulled out a sandwich. He handed it to his dad and took the other one for himself. Peeling back the wrapper, Sam inspected the sandwich. He was pleased to find that it was turkey and tomato with cucumbers and mayo, which wasn't terrible. "So remind me again who this dead dude was?" Sam asked, after he had his first bite.

His dad turned the radio down. They had been listening to the broadcast of a baseball game, but their team was down eight runs, so they'd both stopped paying attention.

"The 'dead dude' was Gregory Vincent," his dad said. "He used to make horror movies in the old black and white days."

"What were they about?"

"The usual horror stuff. Vampires, werewolves, mummies. They were all just people in rubber suits and latex masks, but as a kid, I thought they were terrifying."

Sam took a giant bite of his sandwich, then wiped his shaggy, wind-blown brown hair out of his eyes. "When did he die?" he asked in a muffled voice as he chewed.

"About four months ago," his dad answered. "His estate is clearing out some things. So of course I jumped at the chance to buy what I could. Spent way too much money, too." He turned to Sam. "Don't tell your mom," he added under his breath.

Sam mimicked zipping his lips.

"That's my boy," his dad said, capping off the conversation with a bite of his sandwich.

There was still almost an hour left in the drive. They rode along with the radio turned back up, listening as their team made a comeback. Sam rested his head on the seat back, closed his eyes, and dozed off, enjoying the peaceful ride.

Before Sam knew it, he felt the truck slowing. "Here we are," his dad said, turning onto a gravel drive. Sam rubbed his eyes and shook his head to help him wake up.

It seemed to Sam like exactly the type of home an eccentric film director would own — an ivy-covered brick house in the middle of nowhere, surrounded by a thick, black wrought-iron fence and massive oak trees. The branches draped over the roof of the house, shrouding it in shadows.

As they drove closer to the house, Sam noticed a stone gargoyle with a wide, menacing smile perched on the slanted roof. The monster seemed to be staring at him. As they coasted past its gaze, Sam shivered. The place totally creeped him out.

A black luxury car was parked out front, gleaming in the sunlight. Two women stood next to it. At first, Sam thought that he was seeing double. Then he realized the women were twins who both wore the same black dress, the same wide-brimmed sun hat, and the same sunglasses.

Sam's dad parked the truck, and the two of them climbed out.

"Good afternoon," one of the ladies said. She held out a ring-covered hand, and Sam's dad shook it.

"Afternoon," Sam's dad greeted them, removing his baseball cap and smoothing down his hair. He crammed the cap into his back pocket.

"You're here for the desk and boxes, correct?" the other woman asked. Her voice was raspier than her sister's, like she'd been gargling with rocks.

"Yep," Sam's dad answered.

"Follow me," the first woman said.

She led the way into the house through a

side door. Sam's dad followed, with Sam at his heels. The second sister came last.

The house smelled of dust, mothballs, and stale cigarettes. The wood floors creaked with every step. Old photos and taxidermy deer heads and birds hung on the living room walls, and the floral wallpaper was peeling and torn. Boxes were stacked everywhere.

"The desk is in the office," the first sister said, pointing to a hallway. "And the boxes you purchased are next to the armchair."

Sam followed his dad down the hall and into the office. It was lined with dark wooden shelves, which were crammed with old books, and film projectors that looked like they hadn't been used in decades.

The roll-top desk was against the wall. It wasn't very large (which was good, because it was just Sam and his dad lifting it and Sam hadn't exactly hit the weight room recently). Sam's dad walked over and eyed the ancient books on a shelf. Even from a distance, Sam could see symbols inked on each of their spines: A diamond framing a star. An eye highlighted with a teardrop. A maze-like spiral.

"Father's personal journals," one of the sisters said from the doorway. "Handwritten, one for each of his films." Sam's dad looked back at her expectantly. "They are not for sale," the woman said, answering the question before it could be asked.

It took a lot of work to maneuver the desk out of the office, down the hall, and outside. By the time they'd loaded it onto the truck and secured it with bungee straps and a tarp, Sam was sweating and his muscles were screaming in agony.

After they loaded the boxes, Sam climbed into the truck while his dad paid the women for the items. Sam grabbed a can of cold soda from the cooler and pressed it against his sweaty forehead.

His dad jumped into the driver's seat. "Buckle up, champ," he said, as giddy as a school kid. He slid his baseball cap on and craned his neck to give the cargo in back one last look. "Oh man, I can't believe I own Gregory Vincent's writing desk." He took a deep breath. "Stay cool, Jack," he said to himself. "Stay cool."

He pulled out of the drive, leaving the creepy house, the gargoyle, and the twins in the rearview.

Sam was relieved.

They rode back in silence, listening to the recap of the baseball game. His dad drove directly to his store, a one-story building with a giant window in front and an awning with a sign reading New To You! It was smack dab in the middle of a long row of shops that included a hardware store, a barbershop, and an ice cream place that served the best banana split Sam had ever tasted.

They unloaded the stuff, taking it through a door in the back to a cluttered storage area. Sam's mom hated the room. She said it made her feel claustrophobic and sneezy.

"Thanks for the help today, bud," his dad said, taking off his ball cap and wiping the sweat from his brow with his forearm. "I've gotta grab a couple things from my office, and we'll be on our way home."

He disappeared into his office, whistling while he went. Sam checked his phone to see if his friends Bashiir and Olivia had texted him. Nothing. He eyed the desk, trying to imagine why his dad felt that this old piece of furniture was so important. He ran his hand over the desktop, down the accordion front. There were three drawers on either side. He tried to open the top left one, and it was locked. Same with the top right. The bottom left, though, was unlocked. As Sam pulled it open, something inside the drawer shuffled to the front.

"Weird," he said, peering down at the item. It was a videotape, the kind that Sam's grandma often watched at home on her VCR. The tape was black, and had two clear plates on either side of the label that showed the magnetic tape inside.

Sam looked up, toward his dad's office. He could still hear faint whistling. A part of him didn't want to touch the tape, wanted instead to tell his dad about it and leave it be. But that wasn't the part Sam listened to.

Sam picked the tape up out of the drawer and examined it closer. On the yellowed, peeling label was something written in shaky cursive. As he read it, chills ran like waves up Sam's arms and down his neck.

The Gaunt Man. Only copy. Do not watch.

CHAPTER 2

Sam stared at the videotape in his hands.

Only copy. Do not watch.

It was probably written by Gregory Vincent himself, Sam thought. Next to the handwritten warning was a symbol of some kind, like the ones Sam had seen earlier on Vincent's journals. Only this one was a triangle overlapped by a pair of slashes.

Sam was sure his dad would want to know about the tape. He was an honest man, and Sam knew he would feel guilty about finding the rare tape, especially if it contained a movie made by Vincent that no one had seen before. It probably wasn't part of the deal he'd made with the director's daughters, and he'd want to give it back or offer them more money.

So don't show it to him, said a voice in Sam's head.

Sam was surprised by the thought. He wasn't a thief. The one time he'd left Galaxy Comix with an extra issue of *The Amazing Spider-Man* that he'd forgotten to pay for, he'd felt so guilty that he rode his bike to the store the following morning and plunked a five-dollar bill on the counter.

The tape, though . . . it felt different. Secretive. Mysterious.

What if I just watch it, then stick it back in the drawer before Dad notices? Sam thought.

That made sense. Then it wouldn't be stealing. It'd be borrowing. His dad could take it back to the Vincent estate, and no one would even know he'd watched it.

Sam realized then, as he stood staring down at the tape and running his thumb over the brittle label, that his dad's whistling had stopped. He heard the office door close.

Without thinking, Sam slid the tape back into the drawer and shut it just as his dad reappeared in the storage room. "It's nice, right?" his dad asked, thinking that Sam was admiring the desk.

Sam nodded. "It's pretty cool, Dad," he said. *Am I talking too loud?* Sam wondered. It seemed like he was shouting, it was so quiet. His dad didn't seem to notice, though. He was busy digging in his jeans pocket for a key.

Sam's dad placed the key into the front of the desk, unlocked it, and lifted the accordion front. It rose with a clatter. "Just think," he said, "of the hours Gregory Vincent spent sitting at this desk with his old typewriter, clickety-clacking out movie scripts." He mimicked typing, his fingers dancing in the air above the desktop. "Brilliant."

His dad began to examine the desk closer then, using the key to unlock the top drawers and search them. They were all empty. Fear crept into Sam as he thought about his dad finding the tape before he had a chance to watch it, the missed opportunity of seeing something so secret.

His dad reached for the bottom drawer.

"Dad!" Sam said, abruptly moving past his dad, toward the boxes that sat on the opposite side of the desk. "What's in these?"

His dad's hand hovered at the drawer handle, his fingers millimeters from touching it. Then he pulled away. "Kid, you're gonna love it," he said, closing and locking the desk front and forgetting the drawer with the hidden videotape.

Sam's dad opened the top box, reached in, and pulled out a rubber mask. It looked like a cross between a bee and a zombie. "An original mask from *Insectizoid* — one of my all-time favorite movies," his dad said, holding up the ugly mask. Next, he produced a hairy coconut with a thick string dangling from it. "An unused coconut bomb from *Island of Evil*." Next, he pulled out a stack of paper. "The original script for *Fear the Creepers*. Did you know there were only five printed copies? Someone in England paid a thousand dollars last year for one of these."

It went on like this for another box and a half. Sam's dad giddily produced item after item from the films of Gregory Vincent — makeup, masks, and still photos from on set. It was interesting stuff, but Sam was mostly thankful that his dad had forgotten about the desk.

And that he hadn't found the videotape hidden in the bottom drawer.

* * *

"You wanna do *what*?" Bashiir's eyes were saucers. He shook his head. "Nuh-uh. That's, like, breaking and entering, dude."

"It's not if your dad owns the store, dummy," Sam said.

"I'm in," Olivia said without hesitation.

It was Sunday night, and Sam, Bashiir, and Olivia were sitting in Sam's bedroom, huddled on the bed like they were hatching an evil plan. Sam had told them about his trip the day before, about the weird house and the creepy women and the desk with the tape.

"So this tape, it's like . . . a VHS tape?" Bashiir asked.

"Yeah," Sam answered.

"Do you even *have* a VCR to watch it on?" Olivia asked. She sat with her back against the headboard, calm and collected as always. Her lean, athletic legs were crossed in front of her.

Sam shrugged. "I think there's one at my dad's store. We'll grab that, too."

"So you want to ride to your dad's store after dark, sneak inside, and steal stuff?" Bashiir shook his head. "Not cool, man."

"Again," Sam said, sighing, "it's not stealing."

"Stop being a wuss, Bashiir," Olivia said, nudging him on the arm with one foot. She swung her legs to the floor and stood up. "Come on. Let's go."

"Fine," Bashiir grumbled.

"That's the spirit," Olivia said with a smile.

In the living room, Sam's parents and six-year-old brother, Alex, were watching cartoons on television. Alex had a slew of colorful plastic bricks in a pile in front of him and was creating some kind of strange vehicle.

"Look, Sam!" Alex said, twisting on the rug to show off his masterpiece, something that looked like a cross between a fire truck and a rocket ship. "It even fires missiles! Pew! Pew!" He threw a small plastic brick across the room at Sam.

Sam caught it. "Ah, I'm hit!" he said, pretending to be injured.

Alex laughed.

"We're going for a bike ride," Sam told his parents. "Back in a bit."

"Be careful out there," his mom said. "It's getting dark. And it's a school night."

"That's what I said," Bashiir grumbled.

Olivia elbowed him in the ribs.

"Got it, Mom," Sam said.

As the trio walked through the kitchen toward the back door, they passed a series of hooks beneath one of the cupboards. A variety of keys hung from the hooks.

Sam checked to see if his parents were looking, then quickly and quietly snagged the keys to New To You.

The sun was beginning to dip below the horizon. The sky looked bruised and orange. Despite that, it was still muggy and hot out.

The three friends had dropped their bikes in the backyard earlier, and they still lay there beside one another like fallen soldiers. Sam quickly hopped onto his bike as Bashiir and Olivia struggled to separate theirs.

But Sam didn't wait. He had to get away before his dad noticed the keys were missing.

As he made his way down the alley, Sam heard music — heavy metal screaming. He knew exactly where it was coming from: Hudson Laudner's garage.

Hudson was two years older than Sam and his friends, but he had changed schools and repeated grades more than once. He was the only kid in his class to have his driver's license, and he even owned a salvaged hunk of scrap he called a car. He was always out in the garage repairing it. The thing never seemed to work.

Sure enough, light fell on the cement in front of the open garage. Hudson was at work on his car. As though he could sense the three friends pedaling closer, he stepped out of the garage and blocked their way.

"What's up?" he asked, his tone less than pleasant. He wore oil-stained jeans, a dirty white T-shirt, and a red baseball cap that matted down his wavy, jet-black hair.

Startled, Sam brought his bike to a skidding stop. Loose stones kicked up from the back wheel.

"None of your business," Bashiir, who had finally caught up, said.

"Looks like a pack of nerds on a mission," Hudson said. "Where are you off to?"

Olivia glided up beside Sam, using her feet to push her forward. "Leave us alone, Hud," she said.

Hudson had always had a crush on Olivia, something Sam found out during the brief interactions he'd had with his neighbor. Hudson always asked about her, what she liked, if she was dating anyone. He also never seemed to mind that she called him "Hud." It didn't take a rocket scientist to figure out Hudson was crushing on Olivia.

"Yeah, whatever," Hudson said, moving aside. He sounded suspicious.

Sam and his friends continued on their way. They didn't dare look back, knowing that Hudson was watching them as they disappeared down the alley.

All lingering atoms of sunlight had vanished by the time they reached the darkened storefront of New To You. Small pockets of light from streetlamps patterned the sidewalk. Sam biked around to the back and stopped beside the trash cans lining the building. He leaned his bike against one and dug the keys out of his pocket.

"Come on," he said. "We've gotta be quick."

Sam twisted the key in the lock and shoved the door open. A box attached to the wall blinked red and let out a stream of noise. He quickly typed in a six-digit code, and the light turned green. Then he reached for the light switch next to the box.

Olivia swatted Sam's hand away. "No lights. Someone driving past might see us."

"Oh," Sam said. "Right."

He led the way into the shadowy store. Even though he'd been there almost every day of his life, walking through the dark storeroom was creepy. It felt as though something had drained the life out of the space. He stumbled over a wooden chair and almost knocked over a stack of boxes.

Blue light shone from behind him as Bashiir turned on his phone's flashlight.

"Is that it?" Olivia whispered. She pointed to the desk standing alone against the wall.

Goose bumps washed like tidal waves along Sam's arms and neck. "Yeah," he said, afraid to step closer to the desk, "that's it."

They stood that way for a moment, silent, the desk draped in blue light and shadow. "Um," Bashiir finally said. "What are you waiting for?"

"I don't know," Sam said. He inched forward, acting as though the desk was a wild animal that could snap at any time. He reached out to grip the metal handle of the drawer. For a brief second, he feared it wouldn't open, feared the tape wouldn't be inside, that their whole escapade would be for nothing.

The drawer rattled open with ease. And the tape was right where Sam had left it.

Sam pulled the tape out and held it out so Bashiir's light could illuminate it. "Bingo."

"Sweet," Bashiir said. "Now let's grab that VCR and get out of here." He swung his light over to a shelf filled with electronic relics, where a super-old and bulky VCR sat.

"Nice!" Sam said, closing the desk drawer.

Bashiir passed his phone to Olivia.

"Don't forget the remote," she reminded him. He slipped the brick-sized remote into his back pocket, then lifted the VCR with both arms. It looked almost comical, the short, scrawny Bashiir carrying such a huge machine.

Sam set the alarm next to the door. "Okay, hurry," he said. "We've got a few seconds to get out and close the door before the alarm is active." Then he flung open the metal door leading outside.

He dashed out — and ran directly into a shadowy figure standing in the parking lot.

CHAPTER 3

A rush of wind escaped Sam's lungs as he collided with the mysterious figure and fell to the cracked cement. The videotape flew out of his hand and skittered across the pavement. Bashiir let out a cry of alarm. Olivia, who was closing and latching the store's door, clamped a hand over her mouth to keep from screaming.

"See," the shadowy figure said. "A pack of nerds on a mission. Knew it."

Sam looked up to find Hudson towering over him with his hands on his hips. Even though it was dark and he was cast in shadow, Sam was certain there was a smug smile on his face. Sam's stomach turned to lead. Fear was replaced by panic.

"What are you doing here?" Olivia hissed.

"I was following you," Hudson said. "Obviously."

While Hudson was looking at Olivia, Sam got to his feet and snatched up the videotape, hoping Hudson hadn't spotted it when it fell.

He had.

"What's that?" Hudson asked.

"Nothing," Sam answered.

Hudson laughed. "Yeah, right. You didn't come all this way to bust into your dad's shop for nothing."

"Come on, guys," Bashiir said as he climbed onto his bike. He balanced the VCR precariously on his handlebars.

"What's on the tape?" Hudson asked.

"None of your business, Hud," Olivia said.

"Okay. Guess I'll just drive on back home, maybe stop over at Sam's place and ask Mr. Valentine where Sam ran off to tonight."

"You wouldn't!" Sam shouted.

"Not if you tell me what's on the tape."

"Fine," Sam grumbled. "I don't know. Just some old movie."

Hudson looked confused. "That's it? Some old movie?"

"Yeah. I found it in some stuff my dad bought from Gregory Vincent's estate."

"Who's Gregory Vincent?"

"You've never heard of Gregory Vincent?" Olivia asked. She sounded appalled.

"Nope," Hudson said. He held out a hand. "Lemme see."

"He used to make horror movies," Sam explained, handing Hudson the tape. "Old black and white stuff."

"'*The Gaunt Man*,'" Hudson read aloud. "'Only copy. Do not watch.' Huh."

"Wow," Olivia said. "He can actually read."

"Funny," Hudson said. He turned the tape in his hands.

Sam watched his every move, imagining Hudson's huge hands snapping the tape in two.

"So," Hudson said, smiling. "When's movie night?"

Olivia let out a burst of laughter that echoed through the empty parking lot. "Look who's cracking jokes now," she said.

"I'm . . . I'm not even sure we're gonna watch it," Sam said, feeling hesitant to include Hudson.

"Come on," Hudson said. "You didn't go through all this trouble to not watch it. And I'm gonna be there when you do."

"No, you're not," Olivia said.

"Then Mr. Valentine and I are about to have a lovely chat."

"Okay, okay," Sam said, giving in. "You can watch it with us. Just . . . give me the tape back."

"I'm free Friday night," Hudson said. He held the tape out to Sam. As Sam reached for it, though, he pulled it back, just out of reach. "I want popcorn, too."

Sam lunged forward, grasped the tape, and attempted to pull it from Hudson's oily fingers.

"Let me take the VCR, at least. I'll keep it in my car till Friday," Hudson said as he gave up the tape.

"No way," Sam replied.

"Aw, come on. Let him take it," Bashiir said. "This is gonna be tough to pedal home."

"All right, fine. Friday at 8:30. Don't be late," Sam said.

Bashiir lugged the machine over to Hudson, who took it in his arms and laughed as Sam, Olivia, and Bashiir mounted their bikes. "See you Friday!" he called out as they pedaled away.

* * *

"Whatever you do, please don't eat potato chips and ice cream for dinner," Sam's mom said on Friday evening as she draped a shawl over her shoulders and checked her outfit in the living room's full-length mirror.

From his spot on the couch, Sam rolled his eyes. "Yes, Mom," he said.

"And your brother's bedtime is right at eight o'clock," she explained, as if Sam had never watched Alex while they went out for dinner with their friends before.

"Got it."

"Nine o'clock!" Alex shouted from the floor, where he was lining up his toy cars.

"No way, mister," his mom said, wagging a finger.

"Midnight!"

"Eight o'clock, chump," Sam said, enjoying the chance to overrule Alex.

Their mom walked over and kissed Sam on the top of the head. "Be good," she said. Alex leapt up off the floor, and she gave him a smooch as well.

"Always," Sam said.

Two quick, sharp honks came from the driveway. Sam's dad was already in the car. Their mom whisked her way out the door.

"So," Sam said when she was gone, "potato chips and ice cream?"

"Yeah!" Alex cheered.

They dug into a big bag of chips while Sam microwaved some leftover spaghetti. He and Alex ate while watching television, and Sam checked the time constantly. Olivia and Bashiir had said they would come over at 8:30, after Alex went to bed.

Sam had kept the copy of *The Gaunt Man* safely tucked away in his closet. All week, he'd wanted so badly to watch it.

After pajamas and teeth brushing and about seven chapters of some book about a ninja mouse, Sam clicked off the light in his brother's room, walked back downstairs, and sent out the text message: *All clear.*

Minutes later, there was a light knock on the front door. Olivia's and Bashiir's faces showed through the narrow window that ran alongside the doorframe.

Just as the three friends headed into the kitchen to gather snacks, three loud knocks rattled the front door. Afraid that Alex would wake up, Sam hurried to answer before the knocks came again.

Hudson barreled into the house, the VCR in his arms. "You didn't start without me, did you?" He paused. "Guess you couldn't," he said, peering down at the machine.

Sam shook his head.

"Good," Hudson said, placing the VCR on the floor in front of the TV. Without bothering to hook it up, he fell heavily onto the couch. "Now where's that popcorn?"

Hudson Laudner is in my house, Sam thought. *Weird.*

The Valentines and the Laudners had been neighbors as long as Sam could remember. Yet Hudson hadn't been inside Sam's house since they were very young and he had hit Sam over the head with a toy dump truck.

But there he was, seated on the couch, his feet up on the coffee table as though he owned the place. "This better be a scary movie, Valentine," Hudson said. "Like those Zom-borg movies. Man, I love those."

Bashiir made the connections on the cables, using an adapter that had come with the VCR to hook it up to the TV. Like a doctor asking for surgical instruments, he finally held out a hand and said, "Tape."

Sam passed over the copy of *The Gaunt Man*. He wished his nerves would settle. Worst-case scenarios kept running through his mind. What if the tape got stuck in the VCR? What if it disintegrated the second they fired it up? What if there was nothing on the tape at all?

Bashiir loaded the video into the top of the machine and closed it with a click. He slid onto the couch, where Sam and Olivia had already joined Hudson. It didn't even feel crowded — Sam actually felt safer from whatever the movie might bring.

"All right," Sam said, holding out the giant remote. "Everybody ready?"

Bashiir, Olivia, and Hudson all nodded in response.

Sam pressed play.

CHAPTER 4

Wavy, warped lines in shades of gray and white filled the television screen. The tape clicked inside the VCR as the machine tried to run properly for probably the first time in years. Sam leaned forward.

It's possible that no one has ever seen this, he thought. *Not since Gregory Vincent produced it.*

The lines faded, and the screen went dark, and then flickered. Eerie music began to play. White words appeared against a charcoal-gray background:

THE GAUNT MAN

. . . The title dissolves and the darkness transitions into a moonlit sky. Flecks of starlight and the full moon glow brightly. The camera pans down from the sky to the earth, where headstones are cast in moonlight.

A lone car sits along the graveyard's gravel path, its headlights off. Inside the car, two teenagers sit — a boy wearing an athletic jacket and a girl wearing a polka-dot dress.

"Are you sure we should be up here?" the girl asks. She looks scared as she peers out the window.

The boy acts smug. "There's nothin' to be afraid of," he says "We're all alone up here." He slides a little closer to her. As he does, there is a soft thump *outside.*

"What was that?" the girl asks, skittish.

The boy shrugs. "Raccoon, maybe." He smiles. "Or maybe it's the Gaunt Man coming to get you. Oooooo . . ." He howls like the wind.

"That's not funny," the girl says. She shoves him away and crosses her arms. "The Gaunt Man is just a legend used to scare kids. He's not real."

A shadow passes across the driver's-side window, and the girl jumps and screams. The boy turns, but he's missed it.

"Billy," the girl says, "I'm scared."

"Someone's pulling an awful prank on us," he says, shaking his head. "I'd better teach 'em a lesson." He balls his hand into a fist.

"Don't go!" the girl pleads as he reaches for the door handle.

But he doesn't listen. He grasps the handle, opens the door, and slips out into the night. He can see quite well in the dark graveyard. The moonlight is very bright, illuminating the boy's face as he searches around for the prankster.

"Come out!" His voice echoes in the vastness of space. "This isn't funny!"

Though the boy does not see it, a shadow over his right shoulder moves.

The figure moves toward him. A twig snaps, the teenage boy turns, and —

Ding-dong!

Sam's heart nearly exploded. He, Bashiir, and Olivia all cried out in surprise and looked toward the front door. Hudson was the only one who didn't seem fazed by the interruption of Sam's doorbell. He reached for the remote to pause the movie.

"I got it," he said, standing and walking over to the front door, crushing one of Alex's plastic truck creations under his foot as he went. Sam glanced at the TV. The blurry image of the screaming teenage boy was frozen on the screen.

Hudson swung open the door and greeted the pizza delivery guy standing outside. Sam could see his Zippy 'Za! shirt from where he sat on the couch. A matching red hat was crammed on his head, trying hard to contain his nest of long, curly hair. He watched Hudson reach into his wallet to pay for the pizza with some crumpled bills, then slam the door in the delivery guy's face.

"You ordered pizza?" Olivia asked.

Sam, nervous that his brother had been woken up by the sound of the doorbell, quickly checked the stairway leading up to the bedrooms. The hall was empty. Alex was still asleep.

Hudson dropped the pizza onto the coffee table. "Feel free to have some," he said. "Pizza's on me tonight." He opened the box and pulled a thick slice free from its oozing, gooey prison. Without a thought, he crammed the piping-hot food into his mouth and chewed loudly.

Annoyed, Sam went to the kitchen to get paper towels and plates. Olivia was the first to give in, taking a piece of pizza and saying, "Free food is free food." Bashiir took one as well, though he looked like he'd lost a bet with his stomach about it.

Sam refused to owe Hudson for anything, not even a slice of pizza.

"Can we watch this or what?" he asked impatiently before sitting down on the couch and pressing play again.

. . . "Ahhhh!" the teenage boy screams as the shadowy figure descends on him.

In the car, the girl waits for her boyfriend, her eyes wide and terrified, with no idea what fate is about to befall her.

The screen goes black.

When the image fades in again, daylight pours in through the window of what looks like a laboratory. An older man in a white coat stands before a table. On the table, covered by a sheet, is what appears to be a body.

A young and pretty scientist breezes into the room, carrying a clipboard. "Doctor," she says, "is this the victim from last night?"

"Yes," the man says. "One of the unfortunate teenagers found in the cemetery."

"Have you been able to determine the cause of death?"

"It's most peculiar," he says as he lifts the sheet. The two scientists stare down at something just off camera. "The body seems to indicate that this person was very ill. It's almost like a sickness overtook him, draining the very life out of his body. I've never seen anything like it before in my life."

The woman clucks her tongue. "He looks so sick and pale. If I didn't know any better, I'd be inclined to say our victim looks like he was killed by the Gaun—"

Suddenly, the actors on the screen began to move at super-speed.

"Hey!" Sam yelled. Hudson had somehow stolen the remote and was fast-forwarding the film.

"Come on, man," Hudson said. "This is boring. Talk, talk, talk. We gotta get to the good stuff. The blood and guts. I wanna see the Gaunt Guy up close and personal."

Sam wrenched the remote from Hudson's enormous hands. "The Gaunt Man," he grumbled under his breath.

"What?" Hudson was responding to the irritated looks on all three faces staring back at him. "Like you guys weren't thinking the same thing. This is Snoozeville."

Sam said nothing as he thumbed the play button to resume the movie.

He refused to tell Hudson he was right, but after a while of watching the same people talking to one another, with no visit from the Gaunt Man, Sam was beginning to get bored. He wondered what made the movie special, why it was so secret that Gregory Vincent had written "do not watch" on the label.

What if Vincent was just trying to warn people away from a terrible movie? Sam feared.

After about an hour of watching, the movie was nearing the end. Sam's eyelids began to feel like lead and he could hardly keep them open. It was then that things finally got interesting again.

The young scientist is the only person in town who hasn't become the Gaunt Man's victim. The others have fallen ill, first to a fever, then to fatigue, as they slowly descend into mindless, zombie-like deaths. The scientist is lost, alone in the woods during a downpour, trying to find any other human to help her. Her clothes are soaked and her hair hangs limp around her face.

She staggers forward, clutching her stomach. The bags under her eyes are dark semicircles. A hacking cough escapes her lips. And then she turns, her face a mask of horror.

The Gaunt Man is right in front of her, blocking her path. "Nooooooo!" she yells, followed by a blood-curdling scream.

The evil creature turns, revealing his horrifying face for the first time, all pale and stretched and lined with wrinkles. Where his eyes should be are deep, hollow sockets. He is more ghost than man. He moves toward the scientist as though he's floating.

She collapses to the muddy ground in a heap, and the Gaunt Man steals her soul, draining the life from her by simply touching his shadowy tendrils to her face.

The camera lingers on the horrifying ending for a long moment.

Then the Gaunt Man looks up, staring directly into the camera. It's as if the evil creature can see beyond the framework of the movie, beyond the television . . .

. . . and out at Sam and his friends.

Sam's heart was racing. The hair on his neck was standing at attention. The world around him was gone. His friends were no longer seated beside him. His brother was no longer sleeping peacefully upstairs. It was just Sam and the Gaunt Man, eyes locked in a staring contest that Sam was certain to lose.

They remained that way for what felt like an eternity, until Sam heard Hudson whisper, "Okay, this is pretty freaky." The spell was broken. The world around Sam came flooding back.

Words in white appeared at the bottom of the screen: *"The Gaunt Man was never seen again . . ."*

String music, low and haunting, began

to play. Credits rolled. The first one read: "Written and Directed by Gregory Vincent." A list of names followed: actors and makeup artists and gaffers (whoever they were), and camera operators.

"It didn't say who played the Gaunt Man," Bashiir said, after the last name had scrolled off the screen.

"What?" Olivia asked.

"I was looking for the name of the actor who played the Gaunt Man. It wasn't in the credits."

"You must have missed it."

Sam rewound the tape. Sure enough, though every other character was listed alongside the actor who portrayed them, there was no mention of the movie's villain.

Sam was creeped out. He pressed the stop button and the television screen blinked to black. The quartet sat in silence for a moment.

Then Hudson stood up. "Well, that was thoroughly disappointing," he said, abandoning his pizza box and the rest of his garbage on the coffee table and walking toward the front door. He swung open the door, shouted, "Don't let the Gaunt Man get you!" and walked off, laughing. He didn't bother shutting the door behind him.

Olivia and Bashiir gathered their things and also headed for the door. Sam suddenly thought about how empty the house was going to be until his parents got home. "You guys wanna stay and play some video games?" he asked. "You can crash on the couch."

Bashiir shook his head. "Sorry, dude," he said. "I can't tonight."

Olivia echoed his sentiments.

Sam walked them to the door.

"You okay?" Olivia asked, genuinely concerned for him.

Sam nodded. "Of course," he answered, putting on a brave face. Inside, fear seemed to tingle through his every bone and muscle. "Be safe," he added.

His friends walked to the sidewalk and out into the street with a noticeable quickness in their steps that normally wasn't there. They were trying to act fearless, but Sam could tell they were as scared as he was. He closed the door, and the latch of the lock sounded louder than ever before.

It's just a movie, he thought. *It's not real.*

And yet the way the Gaunt Man had stared out from the screen, it felt real.

Sam took a deep breath, turned — and cried out in alarm.

Alex stood at the top of the staircase in his train pajamas, teddy bear in hand. He rubbed his eyes, squinting.

"What's wrong?" Sam asked, trying to settle his nerves. "Why are you awake?"

"I saw a monster," Alex said. "It was in my bedroom. It crawled under my bed."

This wasn't the first time Alex had talked about monsters. In fact, their mom had made him some Alex's MONSTER-B-GONE Juice. It was really just a spray bottle with water and a teaspoon of glitter. Sam had reached under his brother's bed, sprayed the water, and tucked the satisfied six-year-old back in a ton of times before.

This time, though . . . well, this time was different.

Because Sam was starting to think that maybe there were such things as monsters after all.

CHAPTER 5

Sam agreed to let Alex sleep in their parents' bed until they got home, since he was so spooked. After tucking him in, Sam unplugged the VCR and all its cables, rolled them up, and hid them at the back of his closet. Then he gathered the pizza box and paper towels and tossed them into the garbage bin in the alley. He stuck the videotape in a shoebox and shoved it onto the top shelf in his closet, behind three-ring binders filled with baseball cards. Sam didn't want to see the tape or touch it or even think about it.

All he wanted to do was find a good time to be rid of it. He could sneak it back into the desk and let his dad deal with it. Or he could throw it away. That was probably better, just chuck it into the garbage before pick-up day and forget about it.

Sam couldn't sleep. He woke up sweating five times that night, his sheets tangled around his legs. He imagined it was the Gaunt Man, coming to feed.

After the fifth time, when he was annoyed and certain that he wouldn't be able to sleep that night, he pulled out his laptop and began to search. Page after page of photos of Gregory Vincent came up on the computer screen. The director's thin mustache, arched eyebrows, and glinting eyes seemed to stare back at Sam. It reminded him of the Gaunt Man's gaze. In one photo, Vincent was seated at the very desk Sam's dad had purchased.

Sam read everything he could about

Vincent's films, following link after link to clips, stills, and behind-the-scenes photos.

There wasn't a single mention of *The Gaunt Man*. It was like the movie didn't exist.

* * *

The following Monday, Sam rode his bike to school. He'd slept a little better the night before, only waking up twice. He zipped through the school parking lot, past upperclassmen hanging out by their cars. Sam searched for Hudson's junker of a car, but he couldn't find it.

After locking his bike to a rack outside, Sam shouldered his backpack and walked into school. It was buzzing with activity. The halls and cafeteria were swarming. Sam spied Olivia seated alone at a table, sipping something hot from a paper cup.

Sam hadn't seen either of his friends all weekend. They'd texted back and forth a few times with little notes about the movie, usually followed by a scared emoji face.

"So how did you sleep this weekend?" Olivia asked. Her voice was raspier than normal. It wasn't until she spoke that Sam noticed the dark circles under her eyes.

He shrugged. "Pretty awful. You?"

The answer was obvious. "Total garbage," she said, sipping her tea. "Caffeine, don't fail me now. I have an algebra test this morning."

Just as Sam was wondering where Bashiir was — he was always first to arrive at school, the most punctual and well prepared of the three — the rail-thin teen came hurrying through the cafeteria, looking jumpy.

He sat down next to Sam, who didn't even get a chance to open his mouth before Bashiir blurted, "Guys! I'm freaking out."

"Why?" Olivia asked.

"I had a crazy dream about the Gaunt

Man." Bashiir shuddered as he spoke. "It was just like in the movie. He grabbed me with those long arms. And then he stared me down. And I could feel my stomach turn, man. Like he was draining the life out of me. I couldn't move. I was frozen, even after I woke up. Couldn't shout, couldn't lift a hand against him." Tears were beginning to form in Bashiir's eyes, and it suddenly felt very real for Sam.

"It was just a nightmare," Olivia said. She placed a hand over Bashiir's to stop it from trembling. At first, he flinched at her touch. Then he let her hand rest atop his.

"Yeah," he said. He locked his jaw, tightening his face. "It's just . . . it didn't feel like one."

The first tone of the morning sounded, and around them, students gathered up their things, threw away their garbage, and headed to class.

Sam and Bashiir had their first class together. They split from Olivia, who gave Bashiir's hand one more squeeze.

As they walked down the halls, though, Sam noticed that his friend was shambling along like a mindless, hollow zombie.

* * *

Bashiir's mood did not improve by gym class. While Sam sat on a wooden bench, changing into the smelly T-shirt and shorts he kept in his locker year-round, Bashiir moved in slow, stuttering motions. His face was pale, and he spoke very little.

Sam slammed his locker closed. "Dude, are you all right?"

Bashiir nodded. "Fine."

"You don't look fine. Maybe you should go see the nurse."

"I'm fine. See?" Bashiir stood and shook his head as if to clear it. He forced a smile.

Sam was not convinced.

"Everyone line up under the hoop!" Mr. Kelley, the boys' gym teacher, barked at the class as they entered the gymnasium. The class was split into teams for basketball. Sam ended up playing defense on Bashiir as Mr. Kelley blew the whistle and tossed the ball into the air for the tip-off.

They ran down the court as the more athletic kids passed the ball back and forth. Sam and Bashiir watched as one of them drained a jump shot. There were high-fives and fist bumps all around as both teams jogged to the other end of the court and then back again.

All Sam did was run.

"I don't feel so good," Bashiir whispered next to him.

Sam looked over and saw that Bashiir was paler than ever. "Come on," he said, taking him by the arm. "You need to sit down."

They moved toward the wooden bleachers next to the court. Mr. Kelley's face screwed up into a look of puzzlement when he saw them leaving the game. "Where are you two going?" he asked.

Bashiir responded by bending over and throwing up all over the court.

Moans and cries of "Gross!" filled the gymnasium. The rest of the kids on the court scurried as far away as they could. Sam's own stomach turned when the sour stench wafted up to his nostrils.

Bashiir sat down on the bleachers and muttered, "Sorry."

Mr. Kelley jogged over. "Come on, Bashiir," he said. He stepped around Bashiir's splattered breakfast. "Let's go see the nurse. Must be a stomach bug or food poisoning."

Bashiir nodded. He stood, a bit unsteady, and followed Mr. Kelley out of the gym. Sam watched him go, powerless to help.

* * *

Sam sent Olivia a text between classes. At lunch, the two of them snuck over to the nurse's office to check on Bashiir, but his mom had already come to pick him up. The nurse shooed them away and told them to go eat.

Neither of them spoke with Bashiir at all that night, either. When Sam called, his friend's mom told him, "Bashiir is resting now. I'll tell him you called."

The following morning, Sam waited in the cafeteria for his friend to show up.

But Bashiir was still out sick.

Sam got out his phone, typed *Hey man, r u ok?* for what felt like the millionth time, and waited for a response.

Nothing.

For the rest of the day.

And all night.

CHAPTER 6

The following afternoon, Sam and Olivia decided to pay Bashiir a visit after school. Olivia had a student council meeting to attend first, so Sam killed time by riding his bike home, where he ditched his backpack and grabbed a quick snack. Then he biked to Olivia's house to wait for her.

As he wove between blocks, down an alley, along a winding park path, and back onto a side street, Sam thought about his sick friend. *Mr. Kelley said it could be food poisoning,* he thought. *Or a stomach bug. That's got to be it. It's just silly to think that it has anything to do with the Gaunt Man or Bashiir's nightmare.*

No one was home at Olivia's, so Sam parked his bike on the lawn and sat on the front steps. The street was quiet and peaceful, a cul-de-sac surrounded by thick woods. Sam and his friends had spent many hours running through those woods, pretending to be heroes and villains. A trail wound through the trees. It came out close to the school. Sam kept his eye on it, waiting for Olivia to emerge.

When she did ten minutes later, she was sprinting at full speed, stumbling and staggering. Even from a distance, Sam could see the panic in her eyes.

Sam raced down the steps and sidewalk and out to the street. He met Olivia in the middle of the cul-de-sac when she slammed into him, nearly knocking both of them to the cement.

"I . . . saw . . . him," she panted.

Sam didn't have to ask who.

"He was . . . in the . . . woods." She sucked in air, her chest hitching.

Sam put his hands on Olivia's shoulders, trying to calm her. His eyes scanned the tree line and the shadows within the woods. He could see nothing out of the ordinary.

"Come on," he said. "Let's get inside where it's safe."

"Nowhere is safe," Olivia whispered.

Sam and Olivia hurried up the steps, where she fumbled with the key before unlocking the front door. Sam kept peering over his shoulder at the shadows, waiting for something to lunge out at them.

Olivia rushed over to the large living room window that looked out on the front yard and the street. She forcefully pulled the curtains closed, draping the room in a hazy darkness. Then she sat heavily on the couch, sweat pouring down her forehead, glistening on the tip of her nose. Sam went into the kitchen and poured her a glass of water from the tap. She drank it in three long swallows.

They sat in silence for a few minutes. Sam perched on the arm of the recliner, watching his friend. Finally, Sam asked, "What happened?" He dreaded the answer.

Olivia said, "The woods . . . it was like nighttime. All the light was sucked out of the trees. I could sense . . . something. So I turned around . . . and he was there. It was hard to see, but I could swear he was watching me from the woods. Coming for me." Olivia clutched her knees and stared blankly ahead as she spoke, not looking at Sam.

Chills crept up Sam's arms.

Olivia shook her head. "We should have never watched that movie, Sam. First

Bashiir gets sick, and now this?" She set the empty glass on the floor, slipped her shoes off, and lay down on the couch. "I don't want to leave. I'm not feeling so good."

"Okay." Sam fell into the chair. "I'll wait with you until your mom gets home."

"Thanks." She closed her eyes and soon drifted off to sleep.

A few minutes later, Sam saw Olivia's mom pull into the driveway. He stood and stretched. Olivia continued to rest, not budging a muscle.

"Oh, hi, Sam," Olivia's mom said as she entered the darkened living room. Her smile turned to a look of confusion. "Is everything all right?"

"Olivia might be getting sick," he said. "Might be a stomach bug. Or food poisoning."

But did he really believe that? Because right before both of his friends turned ill, they claimed to have seen the Gaunt Man.

It's just a movie, he repeated to himself. *It's just a movie.*

"Well, that stinks," Olivia's mom said. She walked over, removed a thin blanket from the back of the couch, and draped it over the sleeping Olivia. She placed her palm on Olivia's forehead. "She does seem a bit hot. I hope it's not contagious."

"Yeah," Sam said morosely. "Me too."

He left Olivia's house and, instead of heading to Bashiir's, decided to bike home. As he left the cul-de-sac, Sam didn't take his eyes off the woods. Even though the sun was slowly creeping toward the horizon and the shadows were lengthening, the sky was still blazing with a brilliant yellow light. Everything looked fresh and new and vibrant with color.

Everything except for the woods.

* * *

That night, as Sam lay in bed watching headlights from passing cars dance across the ceiling, he came to the conclusion: *I have to tell my dad.*

There had to be a logical reason for his friends' illnesses, a sane explanation for Olivia's supposed sighting of the Gaunt Man in the woods. An overactive imagination seeing what it wanted to see? And anyway, Sam's health was normal. Yeah, he was tired and needed sleep, but otherwise, he felt fine. And as far as he knew, so did Hudson.

Still, before he passed the movie over to his dad, Sam wanted to do one thing — something so ridiculous, he knew it was a bad idea the minute it crossed his mind.

Sam wanted to watch *The Gaunt Man* again. He wanted to see the pale-faced villain, to stare him down again and know that the Gaunt Man was just an actor in makeup. Nothing more. Then, when he was satisfied that there was nothing supernatural about the videotape, he would gladly hand it off.

And so, after his parents had shuffled off to bed and he was certain they were asleep, Sam crept out of his room, the bulky VCR in his hands. The tape was balanced atop it, still in the shoebox where he'd hidden it.

It took a bit of time, sorting out cables and quietly hooking up the equipment. He did it in the dark, afraid to turn on the lights, constantly glancing at the stairs and expecting his mom or dad to come down and ask him what he was doing.

When it was all set up, Sam opened the shoebox. Just seeing the tape again gave him pause. *Should I really do this?* he asked himself.

"Don't be a scaredy-cat," he whispered. "It's just a movie."

Sam inserted the tape, waited for it to load, and pressed the play button. He held his breath as he waited for the title to appear, and for the movie to start.

The screen was black. Then came static.

There was no title, no movie. It was gone. Erased.

"What?" Sam's outburst came out louder than he'd intended, and he quickly clamped a hand over his mouth. He looked toward the stairs. Thankfully, no one appeared.

Completely confused, Sam fast-forwarded the tape. It was just static. The movie had disappeared.

"Oh no," Sam said, panic rising in his chest, "What did we do?" He was no longer thinking about the Gaunt Man. He was thinking about what his dad would say if he found out about the tape now. What he'd say if Gregory Vincent's daughters discovered it missing or realized it had been in the roll-top desk and called Sam's dad to get it back.

"He can't find out." Sam held out the

remote, poised to hit the stop button . . . and he froze.

An image had appeared after all, faint amongst the static.

It was the Gaunt Man. And he was staring out at Sam.

Sam leapt back, tripping over the coffee table and onto the couch. He stabbed at the remote, trying desperately to turn the movie off. *It's impossible,* he told himself. *It's impossible, impossible, impossible . . .*

The Gaunt Man continued to stare. His head tilted to the side. His arms reached up, like they could easily slide out of the television screen to grab him.

Sam pressed the power button again and squeezed his eyes shut.

The screen went black.

Sam sat on the couch, the darkness of the living room closing in on him. His breath hitched in his throat and adrenaline coursed through his veins. He wasn't sure what was happening, or what he'd just seen, but he knew he'd had enough.

He ejected the movie, and with the cursed videotape in hand, Sam walked out to the alley and threw it into the garbage bin. Looking down at it once more, the words on its label — *Do not watch* — taunted him for the last time. He slammed the lid closed and wiped his hands, glad that he'd never see the stupid tape again.

CHAPTER 7

Sam didn't sleep a wink that night. Every time he closed his eyes, he saw the Gaunt Man staring out at him from the screen. Or the Gaunt Man following Olivia through the woods. Or the Gaunt Man draining the life out of Bashiir. He tossed and turned, staring at his clock as the red, glowing numbers changed from 12:34 to 1:47 to 3:15 to 5:59.

Finally, as hazy light began to filter through Sam's window, he heard his parents' alarm clock. Sam heard his dad grumbling as he walked down the hall. He smelled the coffee his mom was brewing down in the kitchen.

He heard the quick, thumping steps of Alex running downstairs for breakfast.

Like a zombie, Sam got dressed. He shoved his books into his backpack, threw it over his shoulder, and went down to the kitchen. For the rest of his family, it was a normal morning. Sam's dad read the newspaper. Alex wolfed down cereal while watching cartoons. His mom packed a sandwich and a banana into Alex's fire truck lunchbox.

When she saw him, Sam's mom was concerned. "Are you feeling okay, honey?" She placed a cool palm on his forehead.

"Yeah," Sam said, plucking a slice of toast from the toaster. "Just up late studying. Big test today."

"I hope you didn't catch what your friends have," his mom said. "Olivia's mom called last night and asked if you would bring her homework over. She's been sleeping a lot. Her parents are worried."

I'm worried, too, Sam thought.

He said goodbye, shoved the rest of the toast into his mouth as he climbed onto his bike, and glided down the alley. Lack of sleep had made Sam spacey, and he didn't see Hudson's car backing out of his garage. Sam slammed on his brakes and started skidding, but he couldn't stop. He collided with the rear of Hudson's car and spilled onto the cement, his backpack flying in one direction, his bike in another.

As he groaned and wiped the grit from his scraped palms, Sam heard a car door open, then close. Hudson stood over him, holding Sam's backpack.

"Dude, you okay?" Hudson asked, looking from Sam to his car to see if there were any new dents or scratches.

"I'm fine," Sam said. He stood up on his own and brushed dirt off of his jeans. One of the knees was torn now. *Great,* he thought.

"Still keepin' an eye out for the Gaunt Dude?" Hudson asked, smiling.

Sam snatched his backpack out of Hudson's hands. "It's not funny," he said. "Bashiir and Olivia are really sick. It's exactly like the people in the movie. First they get sick, then they . . . die."

"It's a movie, Sam."

"Doesn't feel like it anymore, Hudson. Vincent warned us not to watch it. But we did," Sam said. "Now we're paying for it."

"Well I'm in tip-top shape," Hudson said, flexing a bicep. "So don't you worry about me, Sammy boy."

"I never do," Sam grumbled. He inspected his bike to make sure the tires weren't bent and that it was still rideable. Then, without another word, he pedaled down the alley.

* * *

Sam spent the morning in a daze,

slogging from class to class but not really remembering any of it. In Ms. Jasper's social studies class, there was a pop quiz about World War II. Normally, Sam would have freaked out about having not studied for the test. But his mind was on other things, so he just circled *C* for every answer.

He decided to visit the nurse's office over lunch and convince her to let him go home. Before he did, though, he stopped at his locker to get his things. He grabbed his backpack, unzipped it, looked inside . . . and found the videotape at the bottom.

"How did it —" he whispered. "I don't understand . . ."

He looked around, like the tape was some sort of contraband he shouldn't have, like he was afraid that a teacher or the principal would see it and confiscate it.

I threw the stupid thing away! he screamed in his head. *How did it get in my backpack?*

The tape looked the same as before, except for a smudge on the label, just below the triangular symbol — a garbage stain.

Sam skipped the nurse's office entirely.

He just wanted to get home.

* * *

Sam spent most of the day in his bedroom, afraid to come out. He felt tired and sick and completely helpless. When his mom brought him a plate of food for dinner and set it on the nightstand beside his bed, Sam's stomach had churned and gurgled.

He didn't eat a bite.

All he could do was think about the tape. Whatever curse was on the film, it had affected his friends, making them sick and hollow. And now it was happening to him.

I have to stop this, he thought. *But how?*

Sam held the videotape in his hands and turned it over, like it might help him find the answer. He ran his thumb over the brittle label. One corner was now curling up, the corner with — the triangular symbol!

That was it. The journals Sam had seen when he and his dad had visited Vincent's home. They all had symbols on them, their style similar to the one on the tape.

I wonder if there's something in the journals that will help me save my friends, he thought.

But the journals were back at Vincent's empty house, miles away. There was no way he'd be able to get there. It was almost dark out, it was way too far to bike, and it wasn't like Sam had a car — or a license.

But I know someone who does, he suddenly thought.

Flooded with new determination, Sam emptied the textbooks from his backpack and shoved the videotape inside. He looked around, thinking about what he could possibly need for breaking into an empty house. He grabbed a flashlight and a pocket knife. Then he zipped up the backpack, took a deep breath, left his bedroom, and headed to the kitchen. He opened the drawer where his parents kept the matches and lighters and grabbed a lighter from it.

When he walked into the living room, Sam found his parents reading and his brother building a giant car wash out of plastic bricks. He didn't stop to talk. If he stopped, then he'd have to explain himself, and he was a terrible liar.

"Where are you off to in a hurry?" his mom asked.

"Gonna check on my friends," he answered.

"Are you sure you're feeling well enough?"

"Yep."

"Okay! Be back soo—"

And like that, Sam was out the back door, heading for the alley, and for the loud music drifting out of Hudson Laudner's garage.

CHAPTER 8

"Dude, you're officially insane."

Sam stood in the open door of Hudson's garage, his backpack slung over one shoulder. He felt like throwing up. Moving fast was messing with his sense of balance.

"I'm not," Sam said, tapping his foot on the ground in hopes of calming his nerves. "The Gaunt Man is real."

"Real?" Hudson said. "He's a character in a movie, Valentine."

"No, he's not," Sam argued. "You saw it. The way he was looking out at us. Like he could see us. He somehow came out of the movie, and now he is hunting us one by one."

"Do you realize how crazy you sound?" Hudson asked.

"He's already gotten to Bashiir and Olivia, and last night he found me, too. It's only a matter of time until he comes after you."

"And you want me to what?" Hudson said. "Drive you over to this dead dude's house so you can rummage through his old dream diaries?"

Sam nodded. "Yeah, pretty much. Will you?"

Hudson mulled it over. Then he shrugged. "If it'll get you off my back, why not?" He slammed down the hood of the car, which made Sam jump back.

"Hop in," Hudson said.

Sam climbed into the passenger's seat, pushing aside clothes and empty fast-food containers. The floor at his feet was littered with soda cans. For all the time and effort Hudson put into making sure his crappy car actually ran, he didn't seem to care to keep it clean.

Sam clutched his backpack to his chest as if his life depended on it. Heavy metal music filled the car as Hudson drove out of the alley and through town. He was an awful driver, distracted and using his knees more than his hands to steer. Sam checked his seatbelt again and again to make sure it was buckled.

The only time Sam spoke was to offer directions. They rode out of the city, onto a two-lane blacktop highway. As they wound through the countryside, the sun was gradually swallowed by the horizon. Soon the sky was shrouded in darkness. The trip was uneventful — just headlights on the highway, bugs against the windshield. It was very different than the last time Sam had traveled this way with his dad.

Finally, Sam pointed to a gravel drive that was nearly lost in the black. "There," he said. Hudson slammed on the brakes and cranked the wheel. He swung into the driveway, then came to a jarring halt.

A giant, black wrought-iron gate blocked the driveway. A chain and heavy padlock were wrapped around it.

"Denied," Hudson said.

Sam cursed under his breath. He remembered the fence, but for some reason he hadn't even considered that there would be a gate. *So stupid,* Sam thought. "We're gonna have to climb over it," he said.

Hudson glanced back at the empty highway in both directions. "Well, we can't stay parked here," he said. "If a cop drives past or someone else sees the car and gets curious, we're busted."

He quickly backed out of the drive and onto the highway again. A quarter-mile down the road, past a field filled with rows of corn that were just popping out of the soil, they found a copse of trees and a narrow gravel path that was really just twin wheel ruts. But it was big enough to pull into and to hide the car from view of anyone driving on the highway.

"Come on," Hudson said, turning off the engine and killing the headlights. The world around them became nearly pitch black. As Sam climbed out of the car, goose bumps prickled up his arms. He turned toward the black, shadowy woods.

He's watching me, Sam thought. He could sense it. Without a second thought, Sam burst into a run, stumbling across the field and toward the house.

"Whoa!" Hudson shouted, chasing after him. "What's the rush?"

"The trees," Sam said, not stopping. "The Gaunt Man . . . I think he's in the trees."

The older, faster Hudson quickly caught up to him. "Chill, dude," he said, grabbing Sam's shoulder and forcing him to stop in the middle of the cornfield. "Just relax. You're okay."

"No," Sam said, "I'm not. And neither are you."

Hudson shook his head as Sam pulled free and continued to trudge through the field. He moved slower now that he was away from the trees, though.

When they reached the wrought-iron fence that surrounded Gregory Vincent's house, Sam pulled the flashlight out of his backpack and clicked it on. He swung the beam toward the fence, searching for a spot to climb over or through.

"It's not very high," Hudson said in a hushed voice. "Ten feet at most." He threaded his fingers together, making a stirrup with his hands. "I'll give you a lift."

Sam crammed the flashlight into his back pocket, grasped the cold iron bars of the fence, and stepped into Hudson's hands. Hudson boosted him up easily, and Sam gripped the top of the fence, pulling himself over and landing softly in the grass on the other side. Hudson easily jumped up, climbed over, and landed beside him.

Sam clicked his flashlight on again, and the two continued on their way.

"Yep, gotta give it to the guy," Hudson said as they approached the house. "This place is super creepy." Sam pointed the beam of light up at the gargoyle perched atop the roof. It looked extra menacing in the glow of light, with long shadows hanging on its nose and mouth and its eyes hidden in the black.

When Sam tried the side door of the house and found it locked, he was not surprised. Unlike the locked gate, he had anticipated this. The house must have been almost a century old. Sam figured that one of the many doors or windows was bound to offer a way in.

He found a boarded-up window at the back of the house, hidden amongst the ivy. "Gimme a hand," he whispered, pressing his fingers under the ancient board and prying it out. Hudson joined him, and together, they snapped the board loose. Cobwebs and dead vines came with it. Sam tossed the board to the grass and pulled open the dusty, broken window he'd just revealed.

It wasn't very large, but the gap made by the open window was wide enough for Sam and Hudson to crawl through. It led to the kitchen pantry, a narrow space that smelled like old spices and cooking oil. Lining the dusty pantry shelves were jars of pickles and sauce, as well as tins of crackers with ancient packaging.

Hudson picked up an unmarked glass jar filled with something that looked about the color of a deep bruise — purple and red. "Ew," he said, examining it in the faint glow of Sam's flashlight. "I wonder if it's brains. Or hearts. Or —"

"It's beets," Sam said. "Pickled beets."

"Oh." Hudson seemed let down. "Bummer. Still . . . gross." He set the jar back down.

In the eerie quiet of the house, every step on the creaking wooden floor felt like an explosion of sound. Sam's nerves crackled with electricity as he led Hudson out of the pantry and through the kitchen. Cupboards were yawning open. With each swing of the flashlight, new shadows emerged and seemed to leap at them. As they moved from the kitchen to the living room, Sam felt Hudson grab the back of his shirt. *He's just as scared as I am,* Sam thought. He felt oddly comforted by the knowledge.

The living room was just as Sam remembered. The animal heads mounted on the walls looked far spookier in the dark, as did the boxes that were scattered like debris. Sam and Hudson wove around them toward the hall. Sam didn't want to linger. He knew where he was going, and he wanted to get there and get out as quickly as possible.

Hudson said nothing as he tagged along. Sam led him down the hall and into Gregory Vincent's office.

For a brief second, Sam feared the journals wouldn't be there. He worried that they'd been boxed up by Vincent's daughters and shipped away to someplace safe.

And then he saw them. "There," Sam said, directing the light toward the bookshelf. Relief flooded through him as he spied their cracked spines. He hurried over to the shelf, eyeing the journals, looking for the triangular symbol from the videotape.

He found it on the journal at the very

end of the shelf. The cover had no title —
just the symbol. Sam plucked the book off
the shelf. "Hold this," he said, offering the
flashlight to Hudson.

Hudson aimed the light at the journal as
Sam opened it and began to flip through
the pages. He didn't know what he was
looking for or what he hoped to find. He
could figure all that out on the way home.
He just wanted to make sure the journal
was about *The Gaunt Man*. Then they'd be
on their way.

The journal pages were filled with the same
looping, careful cursive as the videotape
label. There were passages written in
English, and some in what looked like
Latin. Film frames were taped in next
to sketched illustrations, like storyboards.
Sam recognized the opening scene of the
film, the couple in the cemetery.

The final storyboard caused a wave of
chills to pass through him again. It was a

sketch of the Gaunt Man's face, framed the same way it was in the movie, staring out at the viewer.

Sam flipped the page . . . and found a full-length illustration of the Gaunt Man. It was shadowed with crisscrossed lines of ink and pencil, charcoal sketches that smudged at the faintest touch. In the corner of the page, the triangular symbol with two intersecting lines was drawn in red ink.

"Hey," Hudson said. "Isn't that triangle thingy on the tape?"

Sam nodded. "Yeah," he said, "The tape I threw away last night that somehow found its way into my backpack today. The Gaunt Man is just toying with me."

Hudson chuckled then, the sound so very out of place for their surroundings.

Sam turned to him. "What's so funny?"

"The tape," Hudson said. "It wasn't the Gaunt Man. It was me."

"Wha—what do you mean?" Sam stammered.

"I saw you last night," Hudson explained. "I was working on my car and watched you chuck the tape into the trash. I thought it would be funny to sneak it into your bag."

Sam's heart dropped as he remembered that morning, colliding with Hudson's car, Hudson holding his backpack and offering it to Sam with a smile.

"I was gonna do it at school," Hudson explained, "but then you went and rode your bike right into my car. That was just good luck."

Anger bubbled up inside Sam as he thought about finding the tape and how horrified he'd been at the sight of it. "I can't believe you!" he shouted, closing the journal and shoving Hudson hard in the chest.

Hudson laughed. "See," he said. "There's a perfectly good explanation for all this curse and haunting stuff. Bring the book and let's go home."

The flashlight in Hudson's hand flickered then, and a sound like sharp teeth scraping against wood filled the room. Terror rooted Sam in place, holding him down like his feet were made of iron.

"What was that?" Hudson asked.

Sam couldn't speak.

Towering behind Hudson, his head nearly scraping against the high ceiling, was the Gaunt Man.

CHAPTER 9

The Gaunt Man's face was ashen and empty of emotion. The hollows of his eyes were like inky pools of evil. He wore the same tattered black suit he'd been wearing in the movie. His arms hung at his sides, too long for his body. The darkness of the room seemed to be drawn to him, wrapping itself around him.

Sam's heart thundered in his chest so hard that he feared it would break his ribcage.

Hudson turned, and for the first time, he appeared to be terrified.

"Wha—" he stammered. "What is that?"

"It's the Gaunt Man," Sam whispered. "He's here for us."

The flashlight winked off for good.

The Gaunt Man did not move. He blocked the office's entrance — the only way out. Slowly, his arms rose. They reached out, stretching forward, hands and fingers like crumbling stone.

He was reaching for Hudson.

"No!" Hudson shouted. He stumbled backward, tripping on a box and nearly falling. "Leave me alone!"

The Gaunt Man stepped forward. Shadowy tendrils snaked out of his suit coat and extended toward Hudson. As the Gaunt Man pursued Hudson, Sam saw his chance for safe passage out of the office. Hudson must have seen it, too.

"Sam!" Hudson shouted. "Sam! Get out of here!"

"No!" Sam shouted back.

"Don't be stupid!"

With one final look at Hudson, Sam found the strength to move again. He dashed toward the door, journal in hand. Black shadows clawed at him, trying to pull him back. But Sam was quick, and he raced out into the living room, headed toward the front door.

He fumbled with the deadbolt lock. With a *thunk*, it disengaged, and he swung the heavy wooden door wide.

Hudson's screams filled the house, the world, the universe. Sam wanted desperately to go back, but he knew that he couldn't. It was too late. The only way to help Hudson was to find a way to kill the Gaunt Man.

Sam leapt off the front porch and ran into the night once again. It was more humid than he remembered, and a flash of lightning brought with it a rumble of thunder.

He made it to the fence, began to climb over, and turned back to look at the house. The Gaunt Man stood in the doorway, watching him.

Hurry! Sam's voice screamed in his mind.

Sam pulled himself up onto the fence. The journal slipped out of his fingers and tumbled to the grass. "No!" he shouted. He considered leaping down to get it. But the Gaunt Man was gliding across the lawn now, heading for him.

I have to leave it.

Sam swung his legs over the metal fence and thrust himself forward. He fell headlong into the dirt.

"Oof!" The air was driven from Sam's lungs. He gasped for breath and felt it burn in his chest. There was no time for pain, though. Sam rose to his feet, made sure his backpack was strapped securely on his back, and broke for the cornfield.

He ran in long strides, faster than he had ever run before. Sam was not an athlete — in fact, he hated track and field more than any other sport — but he felt like he was racing in the Olympics. He pushed harder with each step, over clumps of dirt and stone, putting as much ground as possible between himself and the Gaunt Man.

Cold raindrops fell suddenly from the sky like needles, striking his face and clothes. The dirt around his feet was turning to mud. It felt like quicksand trying to pull him down. By the time Sam reached Hudson's car, he was drenched, his soaked clothes weighing him down. He fumbled for the driver's side door handle, praying that Hudson had left the keys in it.

It was locked. "NO!" Sam slammed a fist into the driver's side window. Then another. He wanted to break the window, to get in and get away. Rain coursed down the window and splattered with each blow.

Sam looked back. The Gaunt Man was nearing the edge of the field. He glided above the wet earth, and it appeared as if the falling raindrops were moving through him, leaving him dry.

Sam had no choice — he had to run. He ducked into the dark forest on the other side of the car.

It was cold and damp, but the canopy above kept most of the rain out. Tree branches clawed at him. They hooked his shirt and dug into his arms and scraped against his face. They did their best to trip him up. Sam staggered ahead, not sure where he was going or what he was doing. He could sense the creature at his back.

"Why?" Sam shouted. "Why are you doing this?" He felt hot tears burn the corners of his eyes. He stumbled, striking his shin against a log, and fell hard to the ground. Twigs snapped beneath him like tiny animal bones.

Sam panicked. He peeled off his backpack, unzipped it, dug around, and found the videotape. "Here!" he shouted, holding it out, searching the shadows for the Gaunt Man. "This is what you want! Take it!"

Nothing.

"I'm sorry," Sam said. "I'm sorry we watched it."

He flipped up the back of the video to expose the thick tape inside. Then, without thinking, Sam took the tape in his fingers and began to pull. The tape unwound like a spool of thread. It came out in long swatches, strands of it wrapping around Sam's fingers. The same wrenching sound of teeth on wood filled the forest and made Sam clap his hands over his ears.

The Gaunt Man stood before him.

Sam dropped the tape, searched around in his backpack again. His fingers found the butane lighter. He didn't know what he was doing, or why he was doing it. But there was little time left, and he was out of options.

Sam fumbled with the lighter and brought it out. He clicked it once. Nothing. Twice. The same. Three times.

"Come on!" he shouted.

The Gaunt Man was hovering over him now. His long arms dangled toward Sam, wanting to embrace him.

A flicker of light danced at the end of the lighter.

"Got it!"

Sam brought the lighter down until it was under the pile of tape. Smoke rose from the pile as the tape began to melt.

The Gaunt Man opened his mouth wider than humanly possible and emitted a pained screech that shook the trees and the very earth.

The videotape caught fire, despite the moisture. The small, crackling fire gave off unnatural-looking flames that seemed to snatch the raindrops right out of the air.

The Gaunt Man came for Sam.

Sam raised his arms to shield his face. *This is it,* he thought. *I'm dead for sure.*

Nothing happened.

Peering out, Sam saw the evil creature frozen in place, arms mere inches from him. The Gaunt Man's body burned like the fire, his pale skin flickering and orange light blazing in his black eyes.

Then, as Sam watched, the creature fell apart like embers in the wind.

CHAPTER 10

Sam didn't trust what had just happened. He feared the Gaunt Man would return, so he remained huddled on the ground in the woods, listening to the rain make a symphony against the leaves above him, until the videotape was nothing but a fiery pile of ashes.

Then he stood and kicked dirt at the smoky remains until they smoldered out.

It was still the dead of night, but to Sam, the world had grown a bit lighter. The weight on his shoulders was gone. He was safe.

Sam shouldered his backpack and made his way out of the woods. The driving rain had turned to sprinkles by then, and as he made his way past Hudson's car, a voice carried over the cornfield. "Sam?"

"Hud?"

Sam looked out and, sure enough, Hudson was making his way through the field toward him. When Hudson reached him, he enveloped Sam in a big bear hug.

"Glad you're okay, dude," Hudson said. He was still pale, but at least he was alive.

"Yeah," Sam said. "You too."

"It's gone, isn't it?"

Sam nodded. "I burned the tape. So I think . . . I think he's gone for good."

Hudson placed his hands on his hips and took a moment to catch his breath. "Sorry I called you crazy."

Sam smiled. "Let's go home."

* * *

"Man, it's great to see you."

Bashiir stood at the front door of the Valentine house. Cradled in one arm was a bottle of soda. Sam invited his friend inside, then gave him a huge hug.

"Aww, how adorable!" Hudson called out from his position on the couch. He had apparently already forgotten his show of emotion toward Sam in the field outside Gregory Vincent's house.

It had been a week since Sam had burned the tape and turned the Gaunt Man to ash. When he and Hudson had returned home, he'd slogged inside his house, still wet and muddy, to find his dad sitting at the kitchen island enjoying a late-night snack. His dad had paused, sandwich in hand, mouth open, to stare at the soggy Sam.

"It's . . . uh, rainy out there," Sam had said.

"Everything okay?" his dad had asked.

Sam nodded. "Yep."

He hadn't told his dad about the videotape or about the Gaunt Man. It would be better that way.

That night, Sam slept better than he had in days.

When his dad told him the following day that he had decided to keep the roll-top desk and all of the other Gregory Vincent film props on display at New To You — but not to sell them — Sam had been just fine with that.

Olivia and Bashiir's doctors had no explanation for their illnesses, other than to say, "Sometimes rest is the best medicine." They had both been out of school all week as they regained their strength. Tonight marked the first time they had hung out together since the Gaunt Man began haunting them.

Sam and Hudson had driven back to Gregory Vincent's house one day after school. Sam wasn't sure what to expect, but he was thinking about trying to recover the journal he'd dropped by the fence.

It hadn't been there. And from what Sam could tell, the entire house had been emptied out. The oak tree branches had been pruned to let in more sunlight. Even the gargoyle that had been watching over the place was gone. It had simply looked like a typical country home.

"So are we gonna watch this movie or what?" Olivia came out of the kitchen with a giant tub of popcorn in one hand and a movie case in the other. The colorful cover showed a half-zombie, half-cyborg attacking a group of teenagers.

"The new Zom-borg movie?" Hudson said. "You're a girl after my own heart, Olivia."

Olivia blushed. "Knock it off, Hud."

Sam slid the disc into the player and sat down on the couch next to his friends. No clunky, top-loading VCR this time. That thing was safely back in the storage room of New To You.

As Olivia passed the popcorn over, Sam's dad entered the living room. "Hey!" he said when he saw the group. "How come nobody invited me to movie night?"

"You can join us if you would like, Mr. Valentine," Olivia said.

"Excellent! What're ya watching? A Gregory Vincent film?"

In unison, all four shouted, "NO!"

They all began to laugh. Sam's dad, puzzled, didn't get the joke.

Sam held out the remote and pressed play.

EPILOGUE

Savini, Iowa. Three weeks later.

The delivery man dropped the package off at Reggie's door in the afternoon, two hours before his mom would be home from work. Reggie was playing video games when he heard three sharp knocks on his front door. When he answered it, the brown delivery truck was rumbling off down the street.

A cardboard box sat on the porch. It was all taped up, with one dented corner. The label on the front said it had been shipped from California, from someplace called

The Gregory Vincent Estate. Reggie wasn't sure what that was, but his mom was a film buff who was always buying odd things on the Internet, so he picked up the box and carried it inside.

He felt drawn to the box, like it was begging him to open it, but Reggie resisted the urge. For five minutes.

After five minutes of distracted gameplay, Reggie's curiosity got the best of him. He paused the game again, found a pair of scissors, and carefully sliced open the packing tape at the top of the box.

Inside he found something that looked like a movie or TV script wrapped in plastic. There was also a mask — some alien thing — and at the bottom, a black case. A gold plate on top of the case read: *Property of Gregory Vincent.*

Reggie opened the case. It was used for holding makeup, and was mostly empty inside. Its trays held old bits of colored powders and some worn paintbrushes. There were flecks of fake blood all over.

After poking around a bit, Reggie decided to pack everything back up and tape the box up, so his mom wouldn't know he'd snooped. He lifted the case to set it back in the box and heard something rattle inside.

"What was that?" he whispered. He reopened the case, peered inside, and saw a rectangular item at the bottom.

It was a videotape. Reggie pulled the tape out and examined it.

A symbol — a diamond with a star in the middle — was drawn next to a shakily written title: *Thirst of the Vampire. Only copy. Do not watch.*

"Do not watch?" Reggie whispered.

He immediately grabbed his phone and sent his best friend, Luke, a text message: *Hey! U got a VCR?*

GLOSSARY

claustrophobic (klaws-truh-FOH-bik) — extreme fear of being in small, enclosed spaces

contagious (kuhn-TAY-juhs) — spread by direct or indirect contact with an infected person or animal

eccentric (ek-SEN-trik) — unusual or strange, in a harmless way

gargoyle (GAHR-goil) — a grotesque animal head or figure carved out of stone and used to carry rainwater away from a building

glistening (GLIS-uhn-ing) — shining or sparkling

illuminate (i-LOO-muh-nate) — to bring light to or on something

mimicked (MIM-ikt) — imitated someone else, especially to make fun of them

objections (uhb-JEK-shuhns) — expressions or feelings of not liking or not approving of something

overrule (oh-vur-ROOL) — to reject the decision of someone else

prankster (PRANGK-stir) — a person fond of playing tricks on other people

punctual (PUHNGK-choo-uhl) — arriving or happening right on time

storyboard (STOR-ee-bord) — a sequence of drawings, usually with dialogue or stage directions, representing the shots planned for a movie or TV show

supernatural (soo-pur-NACH-ur-uhl) — existing outside normal human experience or knowledge

DISCUSSION QUESTIONS

1. When Sam found the videotape featuring the Gaunt Man, he knew he had to watch it . . . even though the words "Do not watch" were written on the label. Do you think you would've watched the movie? Discuss why or why not using examples from the text.

2. How might the story have been different if Sam had watched the movie alone? Talk about how Sam sharing the experience with friends contributed to the mood of the story.

3. Have you ever found an object that spooked you? Or have you been to a place, like Sam at Gregory Vincent's home, that gave you goose bumps? Think about a time when you've been scared by an object or place and describe it to the group.

WRITING PROMPTS

1. When Bashiir starts feeling ill, Sam and Olivia begin to worry. Write a scene from Bashiir's point of view after he starts feeling sick. Is he worried? Scared? What does he think is going on?

2. Do you think that Sam and Hudson made the right choice when they decided to return to Gregory Vincent's house to retrieve his journals? Write a short essay describing why or why not.

3. In the epilogue, a boy named Reggie finds a mysterious video that has arrived in his mail. Imagine that Reggie and his friend watch the tape and write a scene describing what happens to them afterward.

ABOUT THE AUTHOR

Brandon Terrell has been a lifelong fan of all things spooky, scary, and downright creepy. He is also the author of numerous children's books, including six volumes in the Tony Hawk's 900 Revolution series, several Sports Illustrated Kids graphic novels, and a You Choose chapter book featuring Batman. When not hunched over his laptop writing, Brandon enjoys watching movies (horror movies especially!), reading, baseball, and spending time with his wife and two children in Minnesota.

ABOUT THE ILLUSTRATOR

Neil Evans lives on the south coast of the United Kingdom with his partner and their imaginary cat. Evans is a comic artist, illustrator, and general all-around doodler of whatever nonsense pops into his head. He contributes regularly to the British underground comics scene, and he is currently writing and illustrating a number of graphic novels and picture book hybrids for older children.

MONSTER MENACES

Whether we believe monsters exist in real life or not, they are successful menaces in the horror genre — and have been for centuries. What exactly is it about monsters in literature, film, and other art forms that terrifies humans?

The English word "monster" comes from the Latin word "monstrum," meaning an unusual occurrence that is taken as a sign that something is wrong within the natural order of things. In the modern horror genre, monsters are often seen as omens — signs of bad things to come.

Some people think Frankenstein's monster in Mary Shelley's *Frankenstein*, for instance, can be seen as a warning not to take the advances of science too far. People who have claimed to see Bigfoot in the wild sometimes see the monster as a sign of death.

Some monsters have features that we associate more with spirits or ghosts, such as the tendrils of smoke-like substance that extend from the Gaunt Man's fingers. Other monsters have body parts or features we perceive as distorted, like the fangs characteristic of vampires.

Because monsters can look so unfamiliar to us, it can be hard to determine if they are alive or dead, whether they are male or female, and whether or not they are human. Their bodies can also transform. One example of this shapeshifting kind of monster is the werewolf, which morphs from a human body into the body of a wolf-like creature. The characteristics that make monsters strange can also make them terrifying. They are not part of a species. They don't often speak. They cannot be defined.

Like Sam and his friends trying to figure out the Gaunt Man, it can be hard to know what exactly monsters are, what they are after . . . and how to defeat them.